NO LO
SEATTLE PUBLIC LIBRARY

COLUMBIA BRANCH
RECEIVED
MAR 14 2013

FAST ASLEEP

in a little village in Israel

Written by Jennifer Tzivia MacLeod

Illustrated by Tiphanie Beeke

It was the rooster that first woke Mrs. Strauss, fast asleep in her little village in Israel. *Who keeps a rooster nowadays?* she wondered. *After all, these are modern times.*

"Kukuriku!" went the rooster, probably looking for water in the dusty grass. Or bugs.

She really didn't know anything about animals,
she just wanted to sleep.

KUKURIKU

called the thirsty rooster.

MeOOOOOWOW

yowled the cat in the yard
of Mrs. Strauss's building.
Mrs. Strauss rolled over
and tried to go to sleep.

Zzzzz, zzzzz

buzzed a mosquito in
Mrs. Strauss's bedroom,
in her apartment in the
little village in Israel.

She waved her hand,
and the mosquito was silent.
Mrs. Strauss shut her eyes again.
But . . .

KUKURIKU

called the rooster.

Meooooow, meoooooow

yowled the cat in the dry hot yard.

Zzzz, zzzz, zzzz

buzzed the mosquito. Mrs Strauss opened the window. (The mosquito flew into a corner.)

“*Sheket!*”

she called to the cat
in the yard. “Quiet!”

Back in bed, Mrs. Strauss rolled over and tried to go to sleep.

Yalalalalalalalala

wailed the radio of the *makolet* man downstairs, announcing that his grocery store was open for business: cool drinks, hot coffee, fresh soft pita. There was no silence here.

Mrs. Strauss pulled the
pillow over her head.
Kukuriku, crowed the
rooster, who sounded
thirstier than ever.
Zzzz, zzzz, zzzzzzz,
buzzed the mosquito.
Meoooooow, meoooooow,
yowled the cat, daring the
radio to drown her out.
Lalalalalalalalala,
wailed the radio.

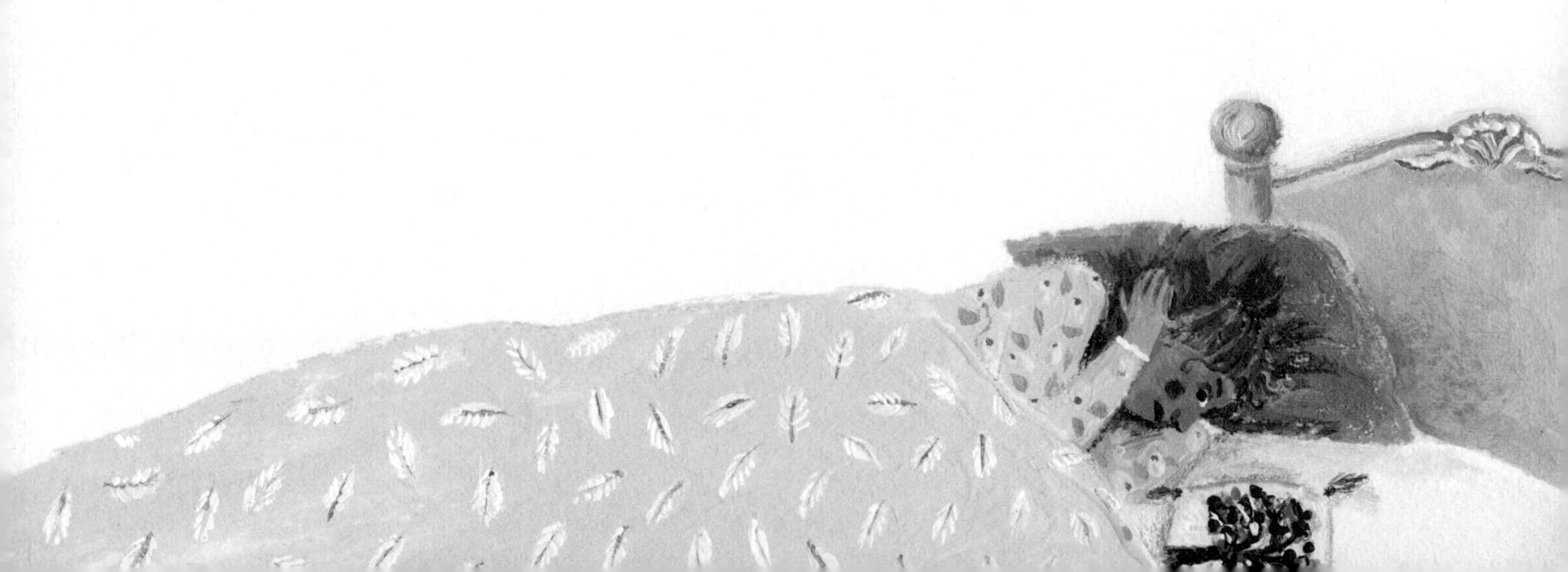

Toooo, toooo,

toooo!

cried the train, swishing past on its way down the coast to Tel Aviv.

The early sun washed through Mrs. Strauss's window, filling her room with light. Soon, it would be time to walk to the school where she taught the children.

But not just yet.

Swish, swish
Swish, swish

whisked the street sweeper, brushing fallen dates, palm branches, and Bamba wrappers off the street in front of Mrs. Strauss's building, in the little village in Israel.

And Mrs. Strauss squeezed the pillow over her ears, covering her eyes to block out the bright sunshine.

"*Sheket*," she whispered. Silence.
A cloud covered the sun. It was cool
under her pillow, like the shade of a tree.

hummed the neighbors' washing machine, in the apartment upstairs from Mrs. Strauss's bed, in the little village in Israel. *Mmm, mmm, mmm.*

But Mrs. Strauss didn't hear it.

Fast asleep at last, Mrs. Strauss dreamed of cool shade, of pomegranates, of the sun on the Kinneret Sea. Of the olives that she would soon help to harvest in her little village in Israel. Of the dry, dry land that needed a drink.

"Shhh," said the young mother, holding her baby close, as she tiptoed past Mrs. Strauss's door down the stairs. "*Sheket*."

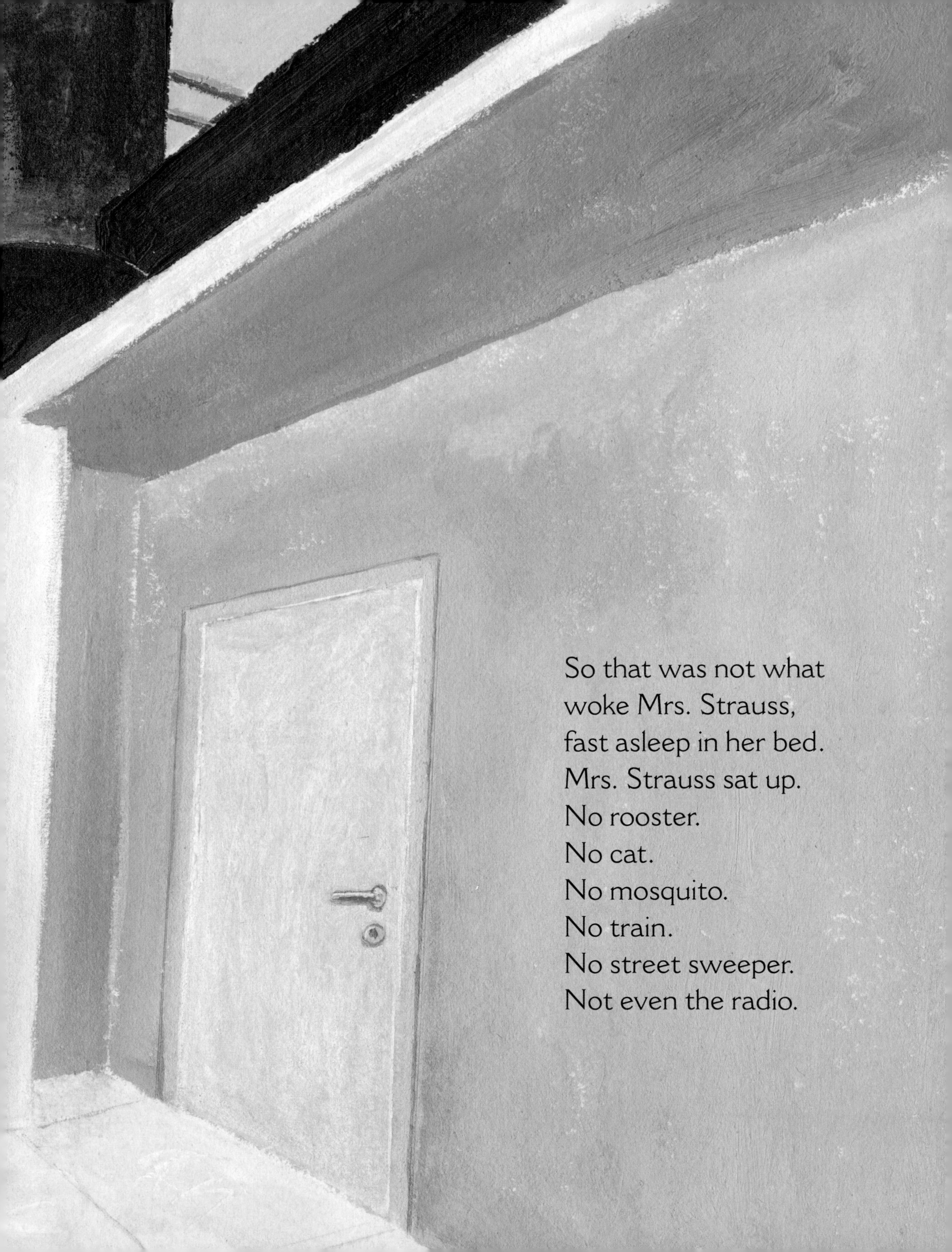

So that was not what
woke Mrs. Strauss,
fast asleep in her bed.
Mrs. Strauss sat up.
No rooster.
No cat.
No mosquito.
No train.
No street sweeper.
Not even the radio.

Mrs. Strauss opened the window
to let in the very biggest noise.

"Geshem!"

Rain. It was raining!
Teef-taf, teef-taf went the
raindrops on the dry, thirsty earth.

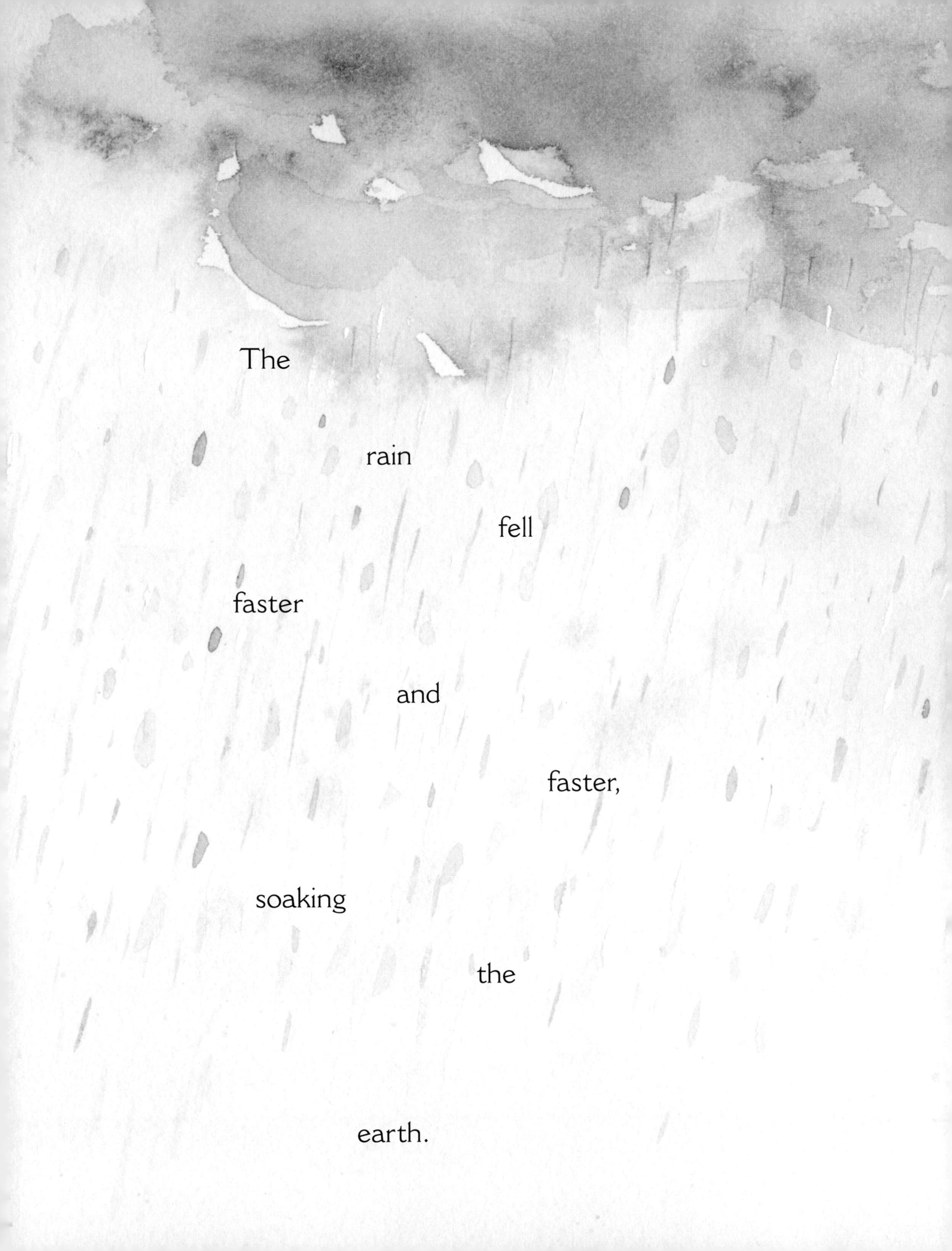

The

rain

fell

faster

and

faster,

soaking

the

earth.

Dignified, the rooster
bobbled home with
one last faint crow:
Kukuriku.

The cat
dodged the
drops, slinking
for cover,
licking water
from its fur.

Mrs. Strauss could hear only the rain, which was splashing all around now. She yawned and stretched as water poured past her window. "*Boker tov*," she said, reaching out to touch the drops. The dry, thirsty world was waking up. She blew the rain a kiss.

"Good morning, *geshem*."

In the closet hung her umbrella.
In the hallway waited her boots.

And outside, a wonderful,
wet new day was beginning
in her little village in Israel.

NOTE TO FAMILIES

I spent most of my life in a place where it rains all year round. So it's been very strange moving to Israel, where—throughout most of the country—rain doesn't fall between May and October. The Torah tells us a lot about rain in Israel, and there are even prayers at certain times of year asking for a good rainy season. The country gets very brown and very dry between rainy seasons. And the first rain is a special occasion, washing away the summer's dust and bringing back the glorious shades of light and dark green, along with bright winter flowers. Next time it rains where you live, ask yourself how you'd feel if it was the first rain you'd seen in six months. Maybe you'd feel like Mrs. Strauss does here—like the whole world, or at least, your dry, thirsty little village, was coming back to life again.

To all our amazing new friends in this little village we call Israel –JTM

For my cousin Richard, who likes cats, and for Amanda, who helped inspire every page –TB

Apples & Honey Press • Millburn, NJ 07041 • www.applesandhoneypress.com

Text copyright © 2018 by Jennifer Tzivia MacLeod • Illustrations copyright © 2018 by Tiphanie Beeke

ISBN 978-1-68115-539-5

All rights reserved. No part of this publication may be translated, reproduced, stored in a retrieval system or transmitted, in any form or by any means, electronic, mechanical, photocopying, recording or otherwise, without express written permission from the publishers.

Library of Congress Cataloging-in-Publication Data
Names: MacLeod, Jennifer Tzivia, author. | Beeke, Tiphanie, illustrator.
Title: Fast asleep in a little village in Israel / by Jennifer Tzivia MacLeod ; illustrated by Tiphanie Beeke.
Description: Millburn, New Jersey : Apples & Honey Press, an imprint of Behrman House and Gefen Publishing House, [2018] | Summary: In a little village in Israel, various sounds have kept Mrs. Strauss awake but when the first rain of the season comes, it quiets everything else.
Identifiers: LCCN 2017025075 | ISBN 9781681155395
Subjects: | CYAC: Sleep--Fiction. | Noise--Fiction. | Rain and rainfall--Fiction. | Villages--Fiction. | Israel--Fiction.
Classification: LCC PZ7.1.M246 Fas 2018 | DDC [E]--dc23 LC record available at https://lccn.loc.gov/201702507

Design by Virtual Paintbrush | Editor: Amanda Cohen

Printed in China
1 3 5 7 9 8 6 4 2

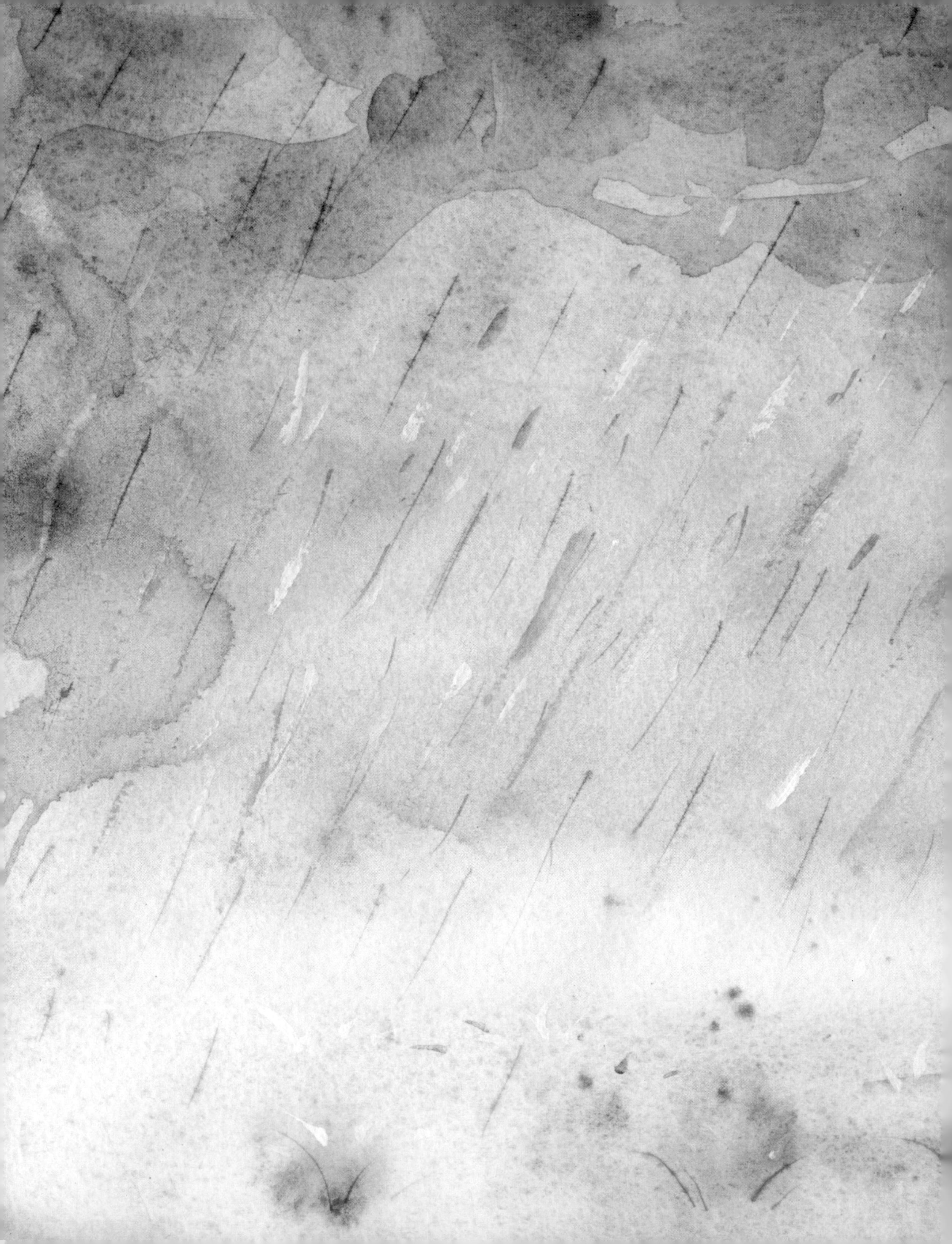